Classic MOVIE
INSTRUMENTAL SOLOS

Alfred
Alfred Music
P.O. Box 10003
Van Nuys, CA 91410-0003
alfred.com

Copyright © 2010 by Alfred Music
All rights reserved

ISBN-10: 0-7390-7009-6
ISBN-13: 978-0-7390-7009-3

Music arranged by Bill Galliford, Ethan Neuburg and Tod Edmondson

Contents

DING-DONG! THE WITCH IS DEAD

(from *The Wizard of Oz*)

Music by
HAROLD ARLEN

Moderately bright march (♩ = 116)

Ding-Dong! The Witch Is Dead - 5 - 1

5131

6

CANTINA BAND

(from *Star Wars Episode IV: A New Hope*)

By
JOHN WILLIAMS

Moderately fast ragtime (♩ = 112)

Cantina Band - 4 - 1
35131

To Coda ⊕

10

CONCERNING HOBBITS

(from *The Lord of the Rings: The Fellowship of the Ring*)

By
HOWARD SHORE

Moderately (♩ = 104)

Concerning Hobbits - 4 - 1
35131

JAMES BOND THEME

By
MONTY NORMAN

18

GONNA FLY NOW

(Theme from *Rocky*)

By
BILL CONTI, AYN ROBBINS
and CAROL CONNORS

Moderately ♩ = 96

Gonna Fly Now - 4 - 1
35131

RAIDERS MARCH

By
JOHN WILLIAMS

March (♩ = 126)

FAMILY PORTRAIT
(from *Harry Potter and the Sorcerer's Stone*)

By
JOHN WILLIAMS

30

32

Family Portrait - 5 - 5
35131

HEDWIG'S THEME

(from *Harry Potter and the Sorcerer's Stone*)

By
JOHN WILLIAMS

Hedwig's Theme - 5 - 1
35131

STAR WARS
(Main Theme)

By
JOHN WILLIAMS

Majestically, steady march (♩ = 108)

Star Wars - 5 - 1
35131

42

IN DREAMS

(from *The Lord of the Rings: The Fellowship of the Ring*)

Words and Music by
FRAN WALSH and
HOWARD SHORE

Moderately slow (♩ = 76)

(with pedal)

In Dreams - 3 - 1
5131

44

SONG FROM M*A*S*H*
(Suicide Is Painless)

Words and Music by
MIKE ALTMAN and JOHNNY MANDEL

Song from M*A*S*H* - 3 - 1
35131

*Enharmonic chord label (instead of A♯13).

OVER THE RAINBOW

(from *The Wizard of Oz*)

Music by
HAROLD ARLEN

Slowly, with expression (♩ = 88)

Over the Rainbow - 3 - 1
5131

Over the Rainbow - 3 - 2
35131

Over the Rainbow - 3 - 3
31

KEEP YOUR STUDENTS PLAYING WITH THESE GREAT PLAY-ALONGS

Arranged for Flute, Clarinet, Alto Saxophone, Tenor Saxophone, Trumpet, Horn in F, Trombone, Piano Accompaniments, Violin*, Viola* and Cello*.

* Piano Accompaniment included

LEVEL 1

Easy Christmas Instrumental Solos
Book & CD

Easy Popular Movie Instrumental Solos
Book & CD

Easy Rock Instrumental Solos
Book & CD

LEVEL 2–3

Classic Movie Instrumental Solos
Book & CD

Harry Potter™ Instrumental Solos (Movies 1–5)
Book & CD

Indiana Jones and the Kingdom of the Crystal Skull Instrumental Solos
Book & CD

Lord of the Rings Instrumental Solos
Book & CD

Selections from Rolling Stone Magazine's 500 Greatest Songs of All Time: Instrumental Solos, Volumes 1 and 2
Book & CD

Star Wars® Instrumental Solos (Movies I–VI)
Book & CD

Top Praise and Worship Instrumental Solos
Book & CD

The Wizard of Oz Instrumental Solos
Book & CD

Visit **alfred.com** for more information

INSTRUMENTAL ENSEMBLES FOR ALL SERIES

Arr. Michael Story

A versatile, fun series intended for like or mixed instruments to perform in any combination of instruments, regardless of skill level. All books are in score format with each line increasing in difficulty from grade 1 to grade 3–4. Perfect for concerts with family and friends, recitals, auditions, and festivals. Available for brass, woodwinds, strings, and percussion.

Movie Duets for All

Titles: Double Trouble • In Dreams • Singin' in the Rain • The Entertainer • Twistin' the Night Away • We're Off to See the Wizard • Be Our Guest • Fame • Wonka's Welcome Song • Wizard Wheezes • Can You Read My Mind? • Star Wars • Everything I Do • I Don't Want to Miss a Thing • Living in America • Gonna Fly Now • Superman Theme.

Movie Trios for All

Titles: Believe • As Time Goes By • Can't Fight the Moonlight • How the West Was Won (Main Title) • If I Only Had a Brain • Nimbus 2000 • You've Got a Friend in Me • Mamma Mia • Batman Theme • Cantina Band • Imperial March • James Bond Theme • Theme from Ice Castles (Through the Eyes of Love) • You're the One That I Want • Raiders March.

Movie Quartets for All

Titles: Hedwig's Theme • Over the Rainbow • And All That Jazz • The Magnificent Seven • Theme from A Summer Place • Eye of the Tiger • There You'll Be • Blues in the Night • The Pink Panther • You're a Mean One, Mr. Grinch • Parade of Charioteers • Hakuna Matata.

Alfred